Mel Bay Presents

Children's Recorder Method

by Sigurlína Jónsdóttir and Michael Jón Clarke

Volume 1

MW00443333

CD contents

2 3 4 5 6 7 8 9 0

Visit us on the Web at www.melbay.com — E-mail us at email@melbay.com

Introduction

The original Icelandic recorder method "Flautað til leiks" was first published in 1995 in Iceland. It has become the leading method for teaching young children music in the public schools.

It was compiled to fill a need based on decades of experience in teaching music in the school system.
We needed music which was **clearly set out**, with **big notes** as many of the students would not yet be able to read, and only one song per page. Any text must be clear and concise and the music must progress in **small steps** so that even the youngest pupils can keep up. The accompaniment on the disc serves many purposes. It makes practice more **fun**, but it also helps **drill rhythm** and is particularly helpful in group work, to keep the ensemble together. Each song is repeated several times, with an introduction and often interludes between verses.

The accompaniments are very **varied in style** and include aural references to both the text and the styles. Use of them while playing encourages listening and playing at the same time. Some humorous aural effects have also been included. At the top of each page is a box with instructions where all new material is introduced, including brief comments about playing the recorder in general. There are line drawings appropriate to the songs which students may wish to color themselves.

When learning each song, it is best to begin by first **reading** the text, and then **reciting** it in rhythm. Next is a good idea to **clap** the rhythm of the song, **sing** the song through and then **play** it. In this way skills have been gradually built up, and the text rhythms help to understand the notes.

Contents

Recorder notes and fingering used in this book

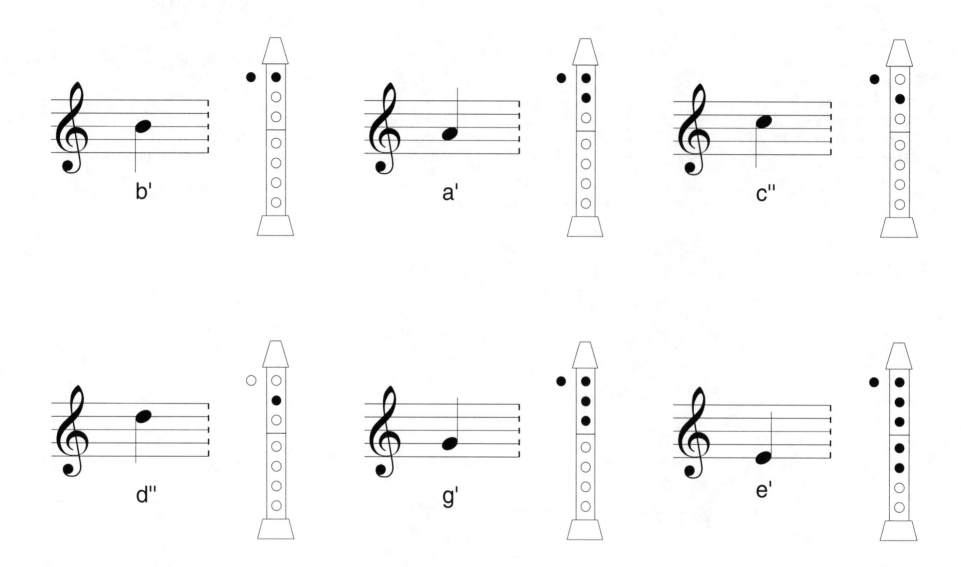

Rules of the game

1. Keep your recorder in the bag when not in use.

2. Don't play and eat at the same time!

3. Blow gently.

4. Don't let your recorder drop on the floor.

5. Don't let others put it in their mouth.

6. Don't chew the mouthpiece.

7. Rinse it out now and then.

8. Listen carefully to the sound you are making.

9. Clap and sing the tunes before you play them.

10. Play for others. It's fun!

–Ready!

Get into playing position, relax your neck and shoulders, and keep a good balanced posture with weight distributed equally on both feet.

If playing sitting down, be sure to sit towards the front of the chair in a relaxed manner, with your back straight and the soles of your feet firmly on the floor.

Begin with the recorder in rest position, under the right arm, with the left hand over the mouthpiece.

–Steady!

Take hold of the body of the recorder
with both hands, the left above.
Rest the mouthpiece on the bottom lip,
making sure that it does not touch the teeth.
Let the top lip rest on the mouthpiece
without gripping it tight.

Left thumb covers the hole at the back
and the first three fingers the first three
holes on the front.

Cover the next three holes with the same
three fingers of the other hand. The right thumb
is placed opposite the fourth finger of the
right hand on the lower part of the recorder.

Now lift all the fingers up except the two thumbs
and the first finger of your left hand. Take care to keep the fingers straight.

–Blow!

Breathe in through your mouth and take care
that you don't raise your shoulders up.
With the recorder resting gently on the lower lip,
close your mouth around the mouthpiece
and blow gently saying at the same time:
DOO-DOO-DOO.

That was the note B.

Now we can play the first song in the book!
It is called "Busy Note B."

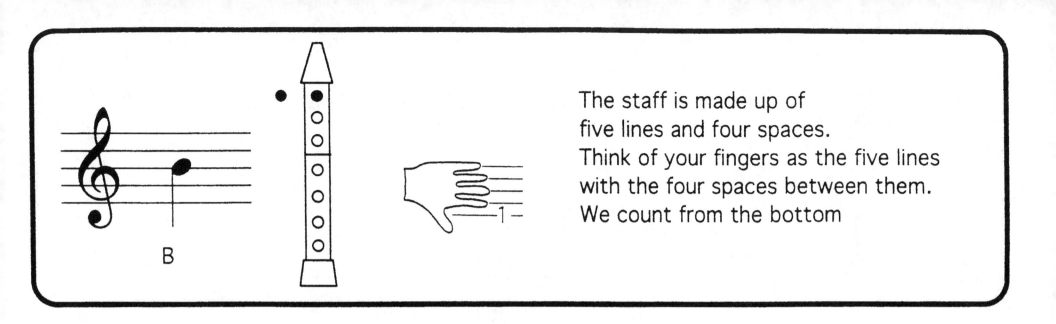

The staff is made up of
five lines and four spaces.
Think of your fingers as the five lines
with the four spaces between them.
We count from the bottom

B

1 Busy B

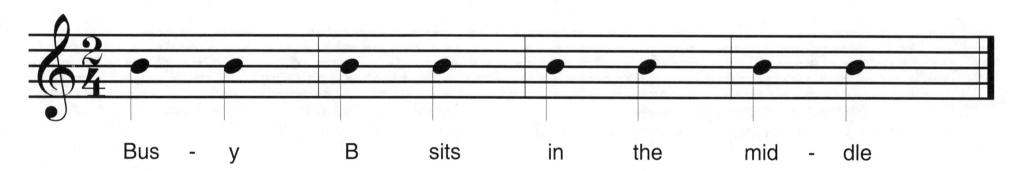

Bus - y   B   sits   in   the   mid - dle

 This is a G clef. It twirls around the line that has the note "G" on it.

 This is a double barline. This tells us that we have come to the end of the song.

2 Knock on Wood

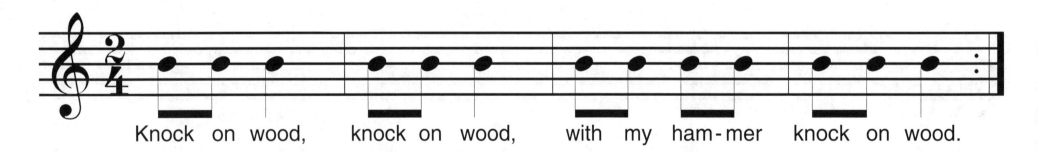

Knock on wood, knock on wood, with my ham-mer knock on wood.

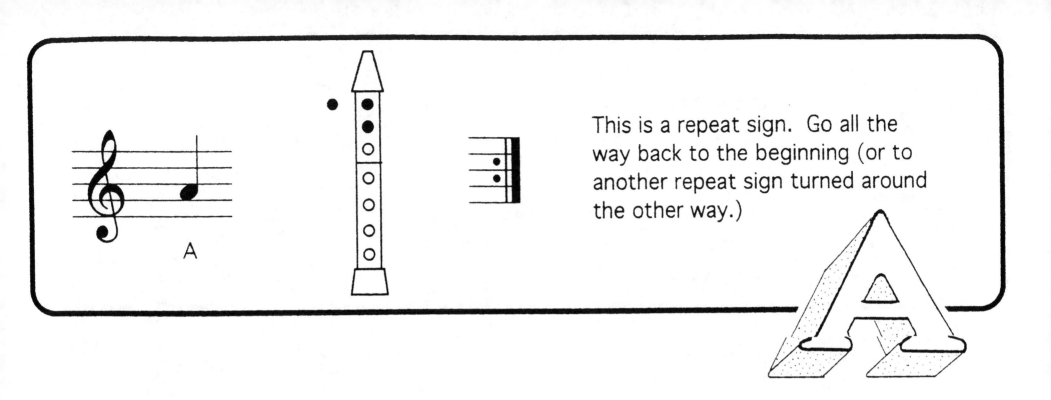

This is a repeat sign. Go all the way back to the beginning (or to another repeat sign turned around the other way.)

A

3 The Note A

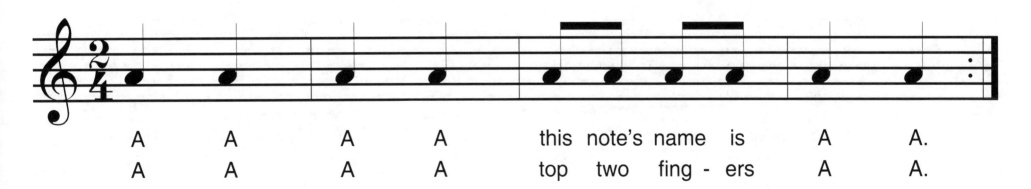

A   A   A   A   this note's name is   A   A.

A   A   A   A   top two fing - ers   A   A.

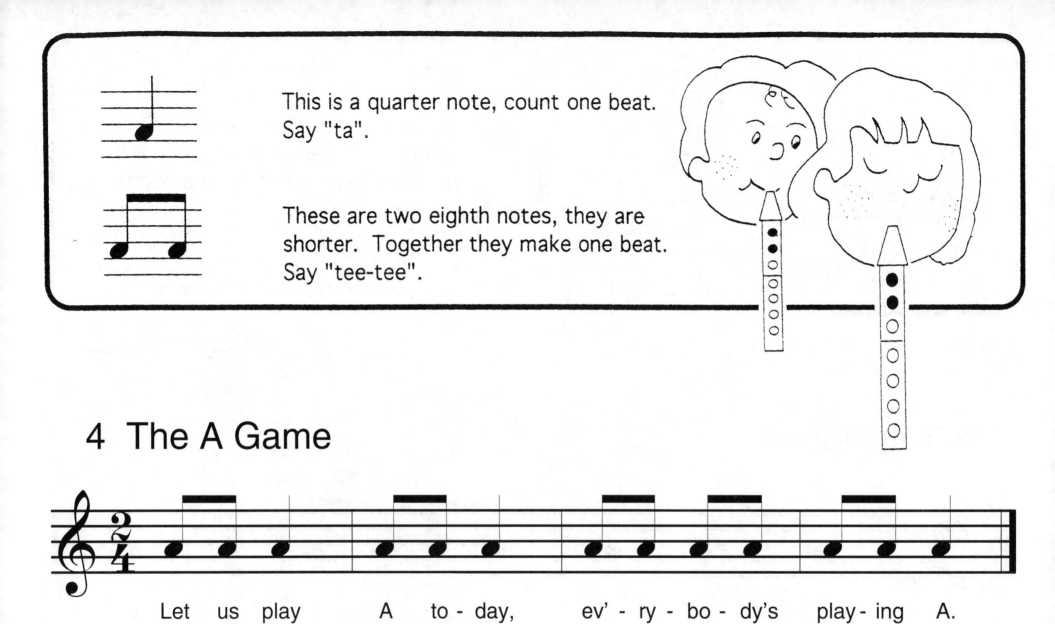

This is a quarter note, count one beat. Say "ta".

These are two eighth notes, they are shorter. Together they make one beat. Say "tee-tee".

4 The A Game

Let us play A to-day, ev'-ry-bo-dy's play-ing A.

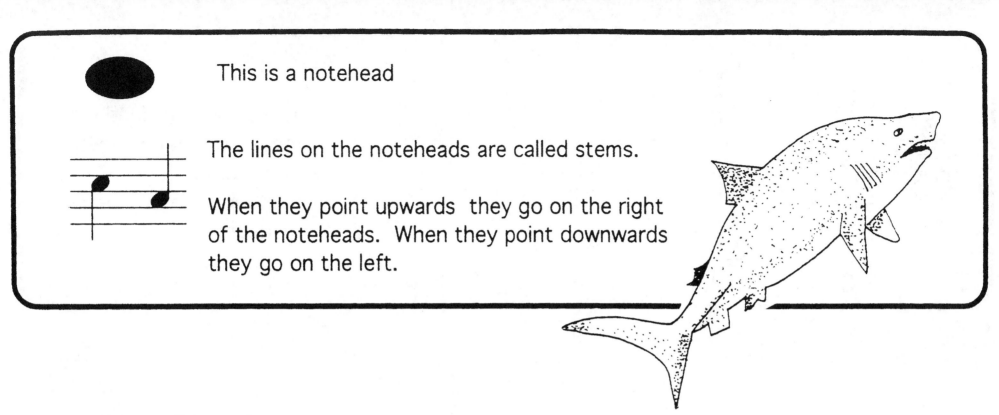

This is a notehead

The lines on the noteheads are called stems.

When they point upwards they go on the right of the noteheads. When they point downwards they go on the left.

5 The Shark

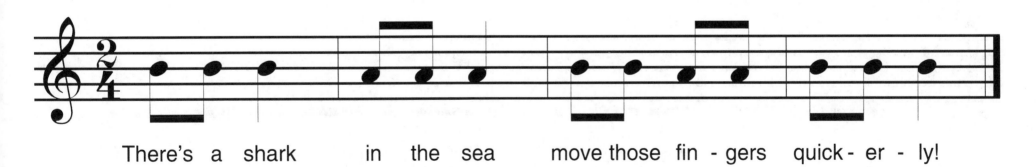

There's a shark in the sea move those fin - gers quick - er - ly!

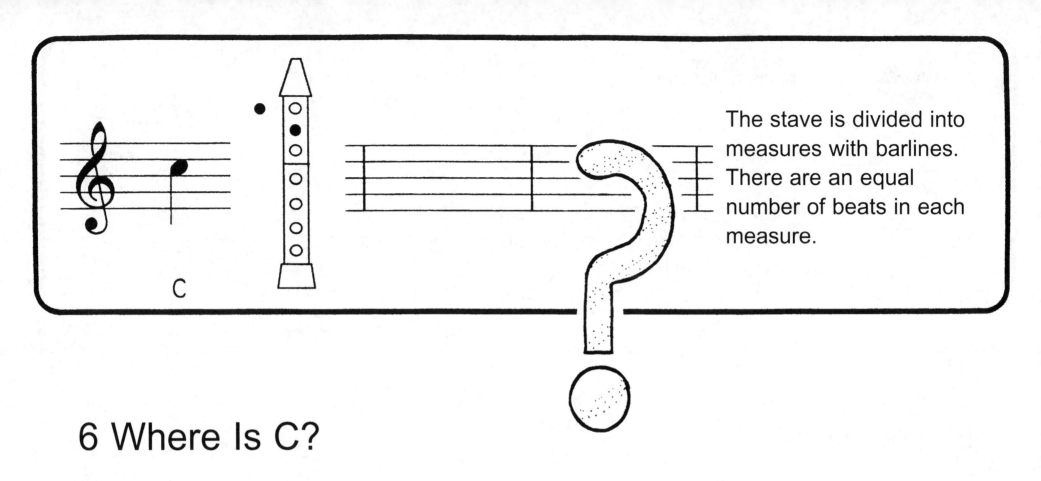

The stave is divided into measures with barlines. There are an equal number of beats in each measure.

6 Where Is C?

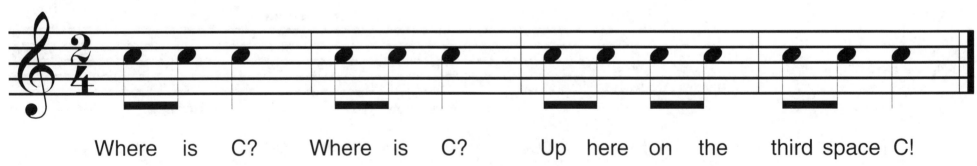

Where is C? Where is C? Up here on the third space C!

Sing this song and clap the rhythm at the same time. Then
we can play the song which uses the notes A and C.

Remember that your tongue says duh-duh...

Listen well to everything you play.

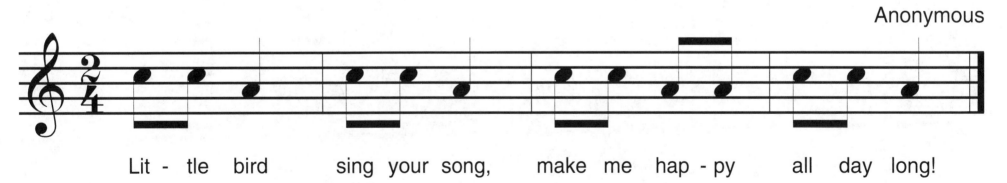

7 Little Bird

Anonymous

Lit - tle   bird   sing your song,   make me hap - py   all   day long!

The numbers at the side of the G clef are called the time signature. They tell us how to count.

In this song the top number is 2, that means count two beats in every measure.

The bottom number is four, which tells us that each beat is a quarter note long.

8 The Clock

Anonymous

One and two and   tick,   tock,   hear the tick - ing   of   the clock.

When the notehead is on or above the middle line the stem points downwards, and is joined to the notehead on the left. Otherwise, the stem points up and is joined on the right.

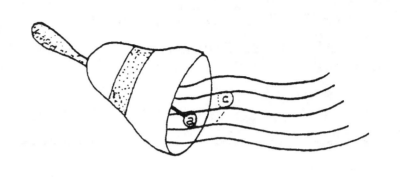

9 The School Bell

Anonymous

Ring the bell now school is out.   Run and jump and   sing and shout!

Remember to blow softly
and try to make a clear and clean sound.

10 Poor Little Daisy

Jón Ásgeirsson

Poor   lit - tle   Dai — sy   feel - ing   ve - ry   la — zy

has - n't   a - ny   milk to - day   all   the   chil - dren   ran   a - way.

Don't forget that your <u>left hand</u> goes on top.

This is a half note,
count one-two.

11 Early in the Springtime

Jón Ásgeirsson

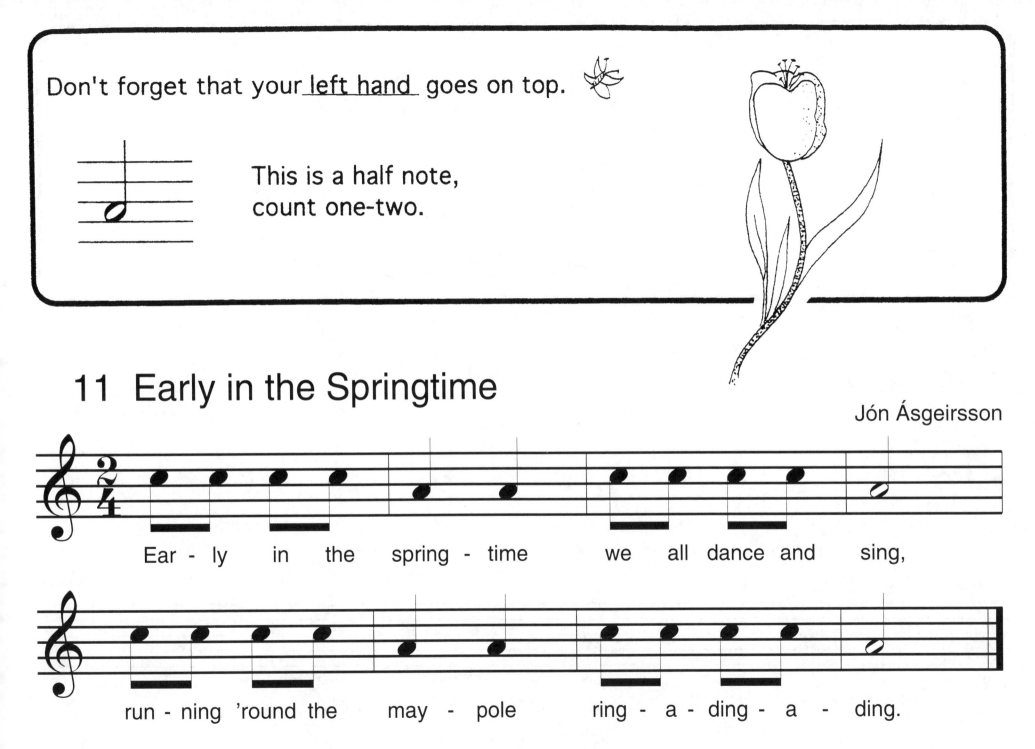

Ear - ly in the spring - time we all dance and sing,

run - ning 'round the may - pole ring - a - ding - a - ding.

Try changing the names to yours and your friends'. Can you make them fit?

12 Home for Tea

Anonymous

Come home Mar - y Ann come home Bil - ly boy.

Come home Pe - ter come on home for tea!

Don't forget to keep your right thumb in the correct place on the back of the recorder.

13 My Little Kitten

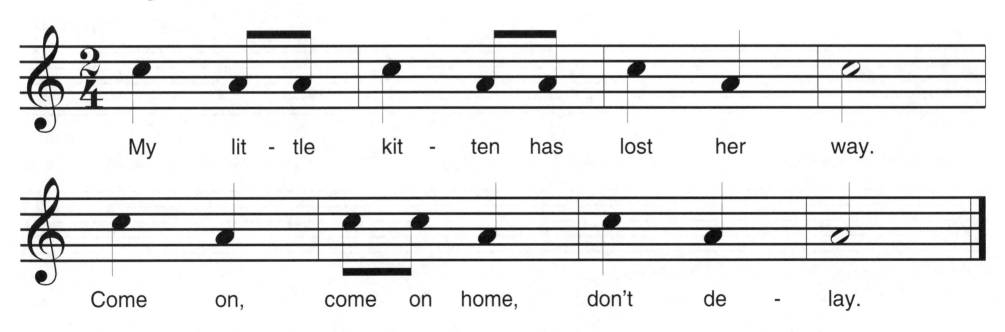

My lit - tle kit - ten has lost her way.

Come on, come on home, don't de - lay.

This is a quarter rest. We stop playing for one beat and say "sah".

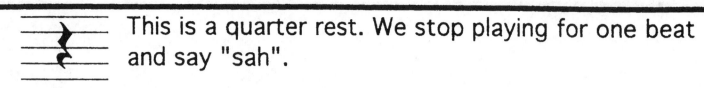 The time signature is four beats in a measure.

Let's pretend we are sailing into a cave, and everything we sing or play makes an echo.
Play the notes loudly (f) and then again in the rests softly (p).

14 Row, Row

Jón Ásgeirsson

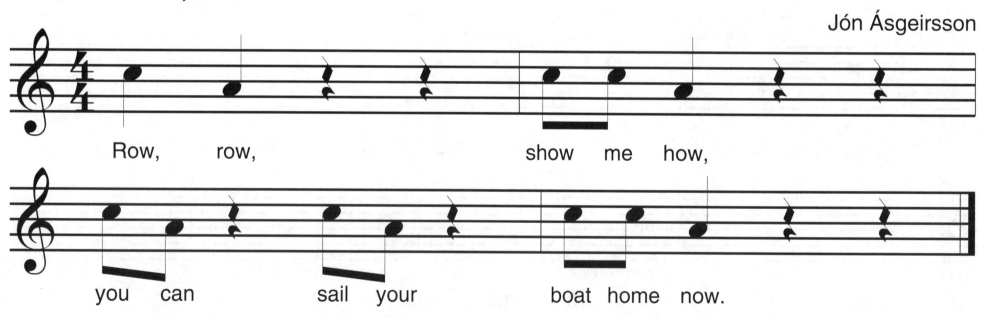

Row,   row,   show   me   how,

you   can   sail   your   boat   home   now.

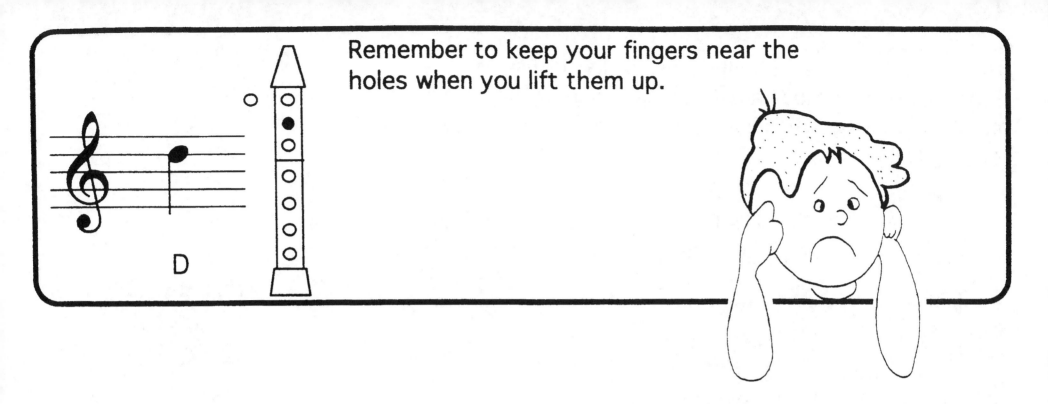

Remember to keep your fingers near the holes when you lift them up.

D

15 Squeaky D

Blow me soft - ly, or you'll see why they call me "Squeak - y D".

Blow gently and make sure the notes sound in tune.
Blowing the D note too hard will make it sharp. Listen
carefully to the accompaniment on the disc and match your
playing to it.

This is a flat sign. It doesn't change any of the notes in
this song, but you will find out more about it in Book 2.

16 Fiddlin' Freddy

Anonymous

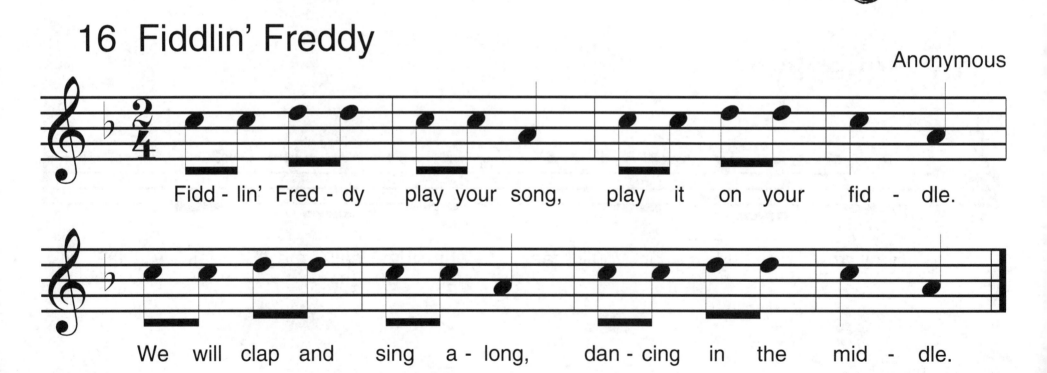

Fidd - lin' Fred - dy   play your song,   play it on your fid - dle.

We will clap and   sing a - long,   dan - cing in the mid - dle.

Get out your recorder and play for your guests when it is your birthday. They'll be amazed at how much you already know.

17 The Birthday Party

Anonymous

Do you know what we will make? We are going to bake a cake.

'Cause it's some - one's birth - day, 'Cause it's some - one's birth - day.

I have got a pre - sent and I hear it say - ing "meow"

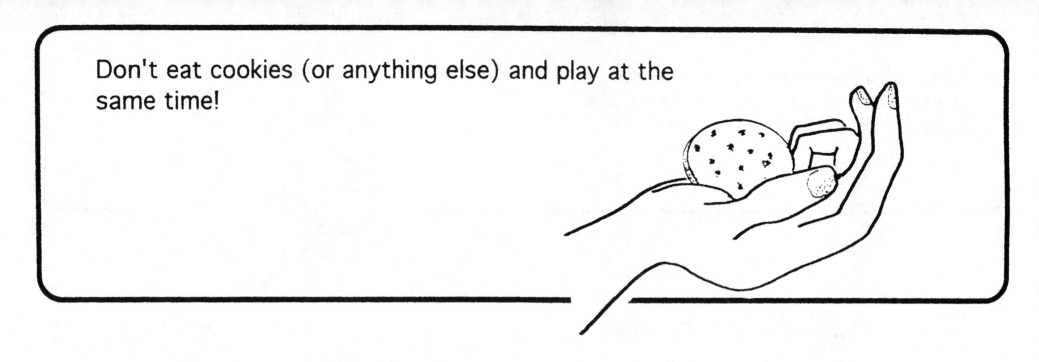

Don't eat cookies (or anything else) and play at the same time!

18 Ring-a-Ding-a-Daisy

Jón Ásgeirsson

Ring - a - ding - a - dai - sy   no - one else must   see.

Pass - a - round some   su - gar can - dy   all   the   way   to   me.

We must dress up in warm clothes for the winter weather. We must look after our recorders, keeping them in the bag when not in use.

19 Pants and Scarf and Shirt and Socks

Anonymous

Pants and scarf and shirt and socks, gloves and boots of lea - ther.

Jónas Hallgrímsson

Cap and coat and wool - ly vest, in the freez - ing weath - er.

Play the short notes like snowflakes landing, short and lightly.
This is sometimes called staccato.

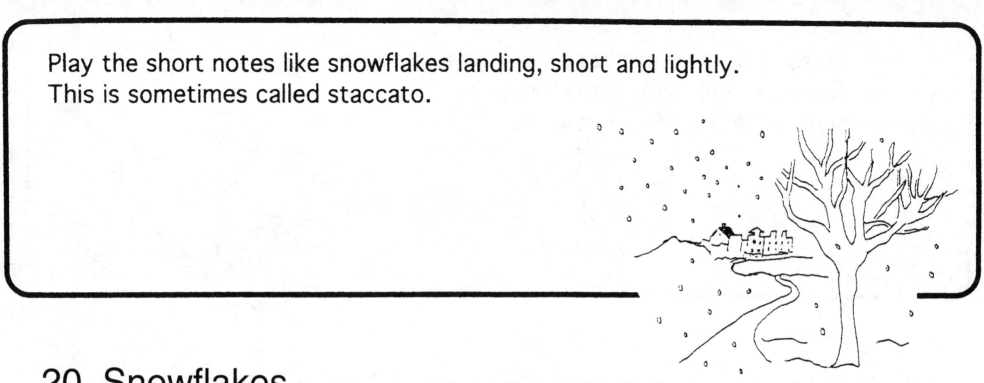

20 Snowflakes

Anonymous

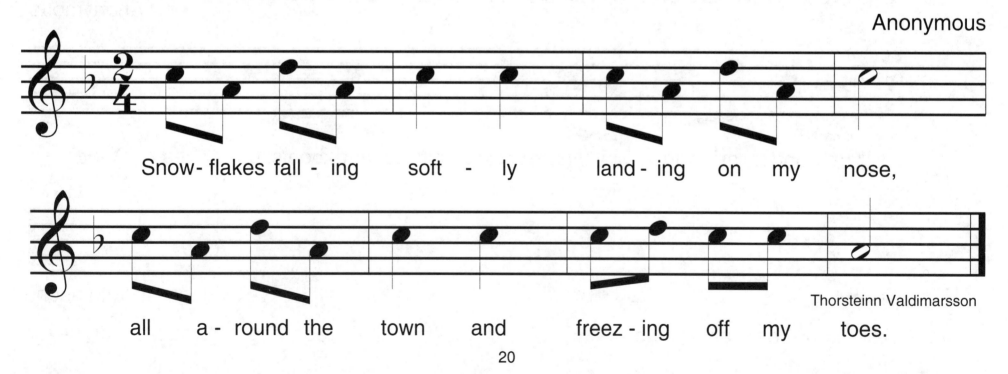

Snow- flakes fall - ing   soft - ly   land - ing on my   nose,

Thorsteinn Valdimarsson

all   a - round the   town   and   freez - ing off my   toes.

This is a whole note, you count one-two-three-four.

This is a whole rest. It hangs below the line like the washing does.

This is another way of writing 4/4.

21 Tootle Rock

M. J. Clarke

We are floo - ters, toot - lin' floot - ers.

Play - ing all day that is our way.

Cool dudes toot - lin' floo - ters.

We can make a soft sound by blowing softly into our recorders. Always try to make a beautiful sound.

22 Softly Sleeping

German folk song

Soft - ly, soft - ly, sleep - ing on the ground,

sit - ting on her litt - le nest, all her litt - le chicks at rest.

Soft - ly, soft - ly sleep - ing on the ground.

G

Make sure that your fingers cover the holes or you will not make a clear sound. Your fingers should be flat, but don't press them too tight.

23 Three Holes Closed

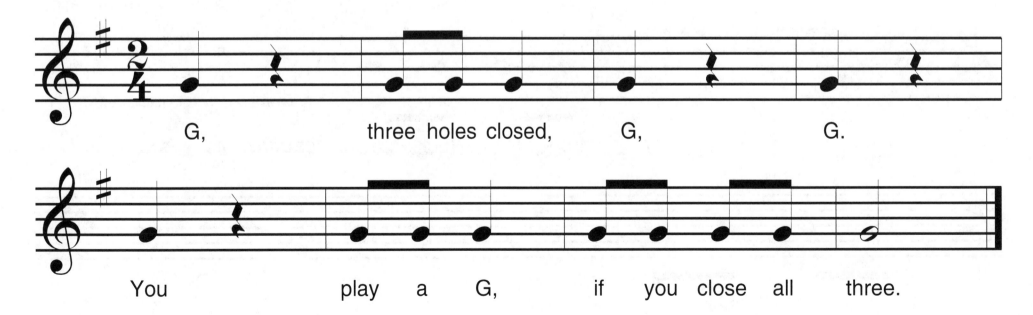

G, three holes closed, G, G.

You play a G, if you close all three.

Be careful not to drop your recorder on the floor like Billy did with his bucket.

24 Little Billy's Bucket

Anonymous

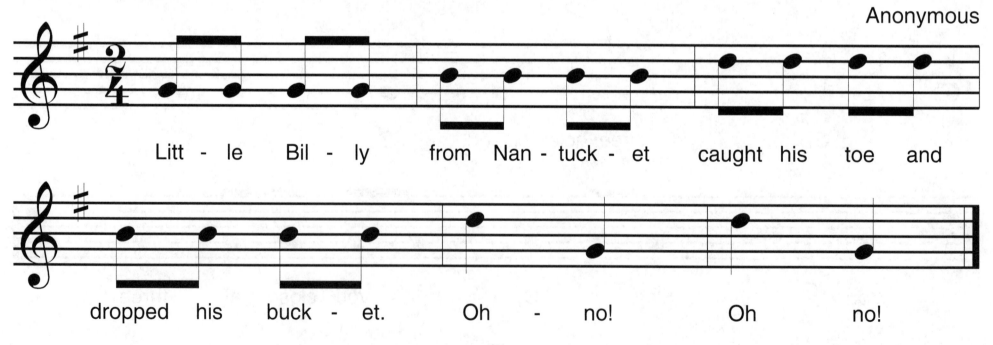

Litt - le Bil - ly from Nan - tuck - et caught his toe and

dropped his buck - et. Oh - no! Oh no!

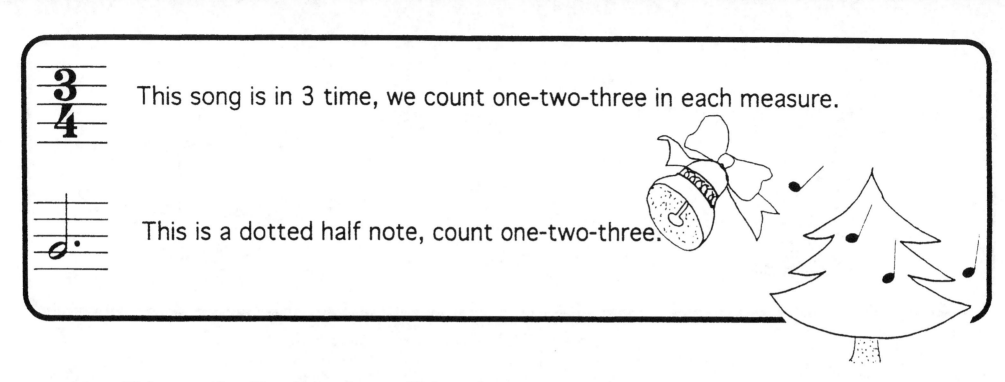

This song is in 3 time, we count one-two-three in each measure.

This is a dotted half note, count one-two-three.

25 Church Bells Are Ringing

Anonymous

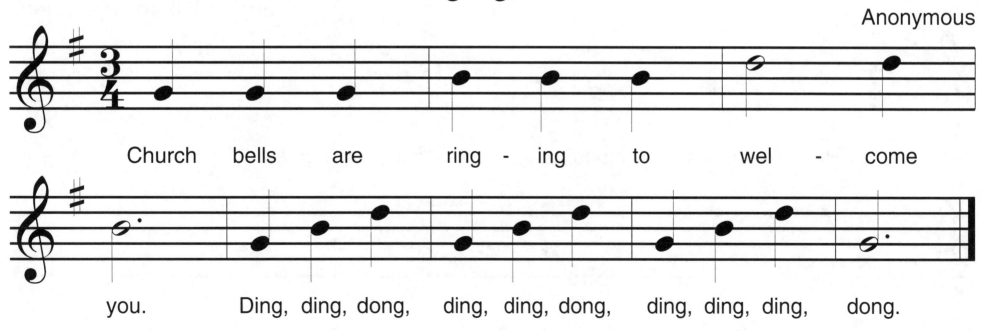

Church bells are ring - ing to wel - come you.

Ding, ding, dong, ding, ding, dong, ding, ding, ding, dong.

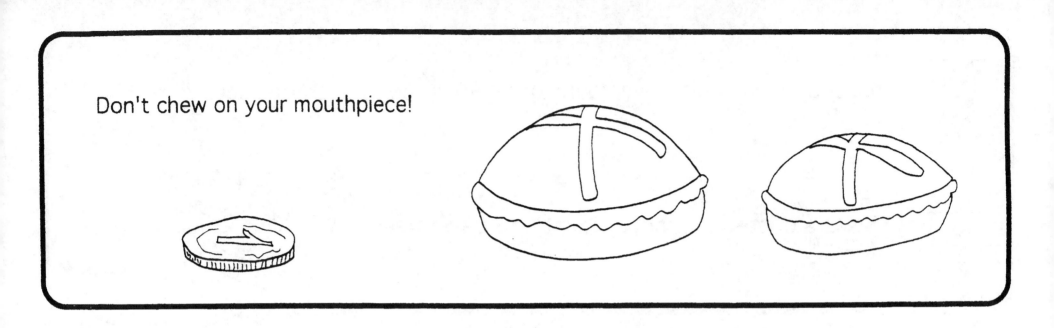

Don't chew on your mouthpiece!

26 Hot Cross Buns

English folk song (adapted)

Hot cross buns! Hot cross buns!

One a pen - ny two a pen - ny hot cross buns!

Notes with dots above or below mean short notes and this is called staccato. Imagine raindrops falling on the sidewalk.

27 Raindrops

Anonymous

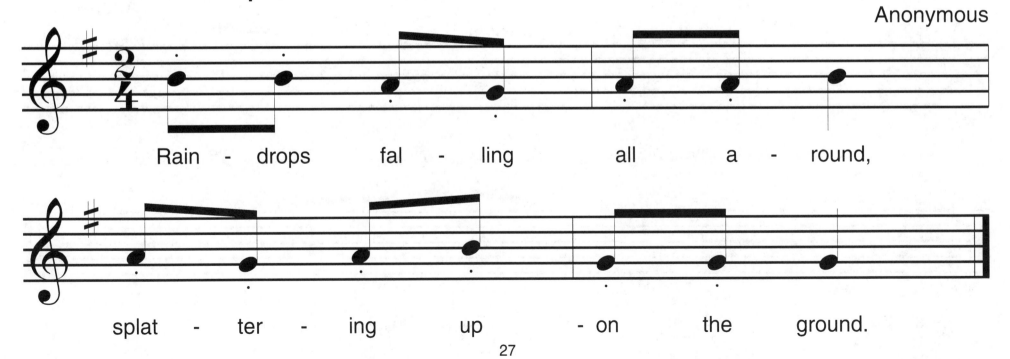

Rain - drops fal - ling all a - round,

splat - ter - ing up - on the ground.

27

Don't put the mouthpiece of your recorder too far into your mouth, and it must not touch your teeth.

28 Rainy Days

Anonymous

Rain - y days please go a - way, so we can go

out to play, run and play all day.

It's a good rule to keep your recorder to yourself and not let other people blow into it.

29 Little Johnny

Anonymous

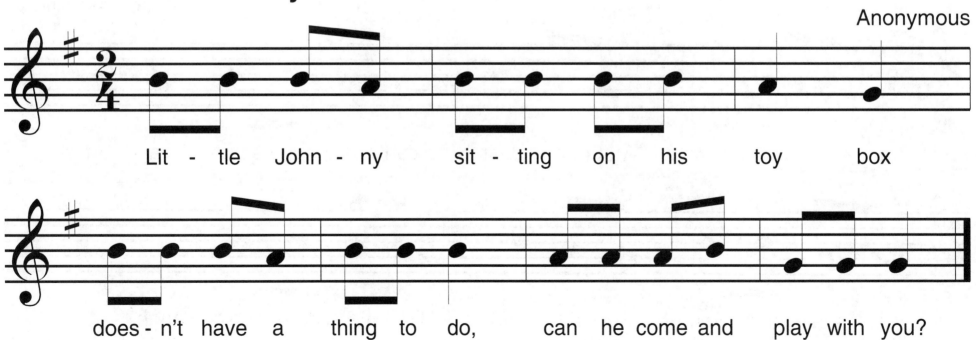

Lit - tle John - ny sit - ting on his toy box

does - n't have a thing to do, can he come and play with you?

This is part of an old Icelandic rhyme, from a time when people were so poor that they often didn't know where to find food for their families.

30 Mother Dear

Jón Ásgeirsson

I am thirst - y Moth - er dear can I have some wa - ter?

I shall give you milk and bread lit - tle dar - ling daugh - ter.

Don't forget to keep your right thumb on the back of the recorder to stop it rocking like a see-saw.

31 See-saw

D. Kabalewski

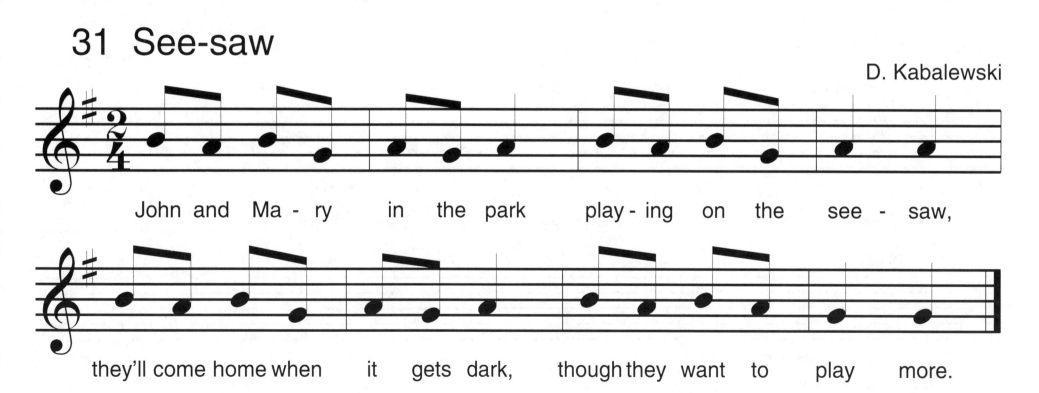

John and Ma - ry in the park play - ing on the see - saw,

they'll come home when it gets dark, though they want to play more.

Remember to tongue properly by saying Duh-duh-duh.

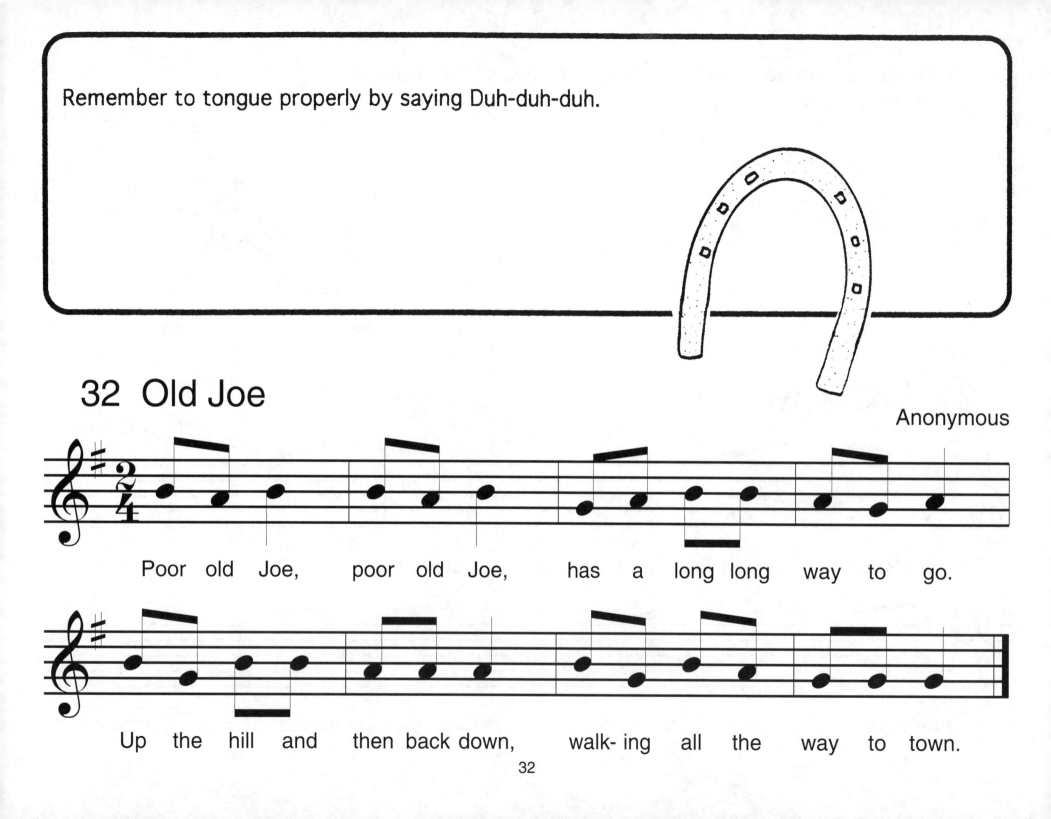

32 Old Joe

Anonymous

Poor old Joe, poor old Joe, has a long long way to go.

Up the hill and then back down, walk-ing all the way to town.

The bar that connects these eighth notes together is called a beam.

Sometimes they are separate like this.

33 G A B

English song

G A B A B A, G A B A B.

G A B A B A G A B A G.

In this old Icelandic rhyme the beat changes from four to three in each measure. This is a form of poetic metre from the Nordic Vikings and is very, very old.

Some modern music does a lot of changing about with time signatures.

34 Clap your Hands and Stamp Your Feet

Icelandic Folk Song

Clap your hands and   stamp your feet   try - ing hard to   keep the beat.

Clap your hands and   stamp your feet   you   are   look - ing   real- ly neat.

This is a fermata. You can play the note under it as long as you think fit.

These notes are tied. You only tongue the first note.

35 Swan on a Summer Night

Icelandic Folk Song

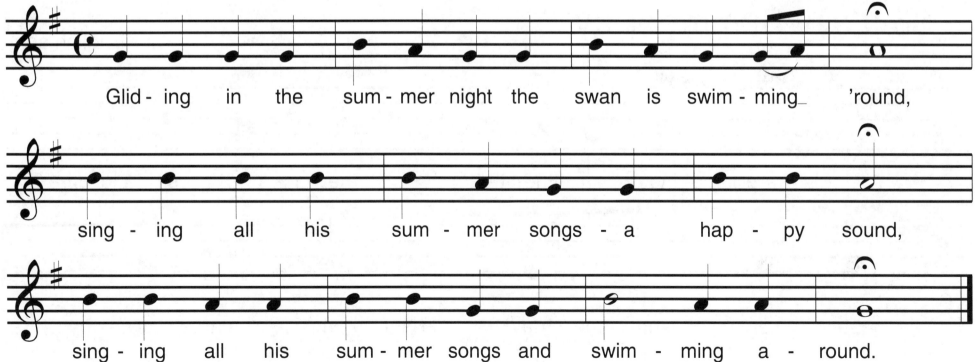

Glid - ing in the sum - mer night the swan is swim - ming_ 'round,

sing - ing all his sum - mer songs - a hap - py sound,

sing - ing all his sum - mer songs and swim - ming a - round.

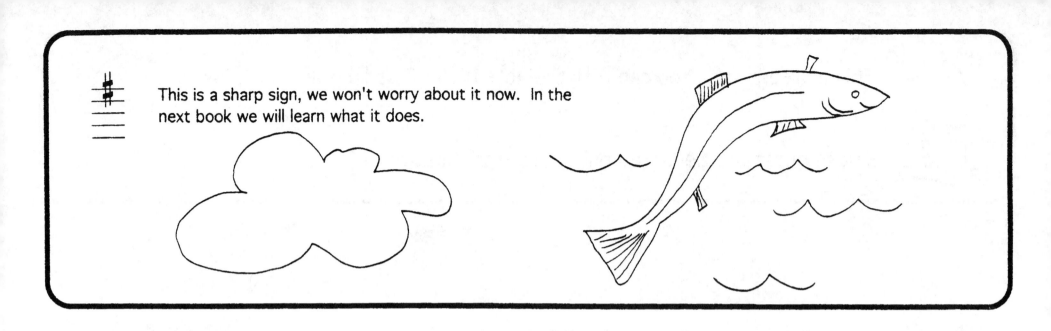

This is a sharp sign, we won't worry about it now. In the next book we will learn what it does.

36 Lazy Summer Day

English song

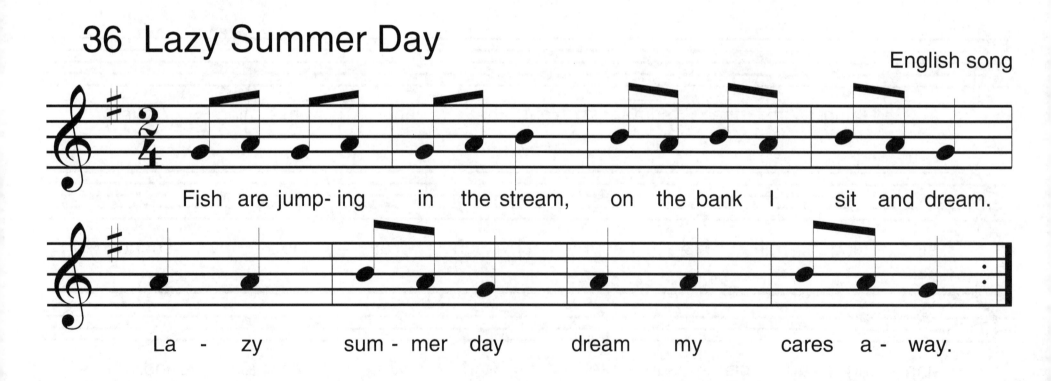

Fish are jump-ing in the stream, on the bank I sit and dream.

La - zy sum - mer day dream my cares a - way.

It's fun to sing the songs through before we play them, both softly (p) and loudly (f).

37 Pretty Birds, Come Sing for Me

Icelandic Folk Song

Pret - ty birds come sing for me, thrush and lark and ra - ven,

while the sun sinks in the sea light - ing up the ha - ven.

Another old Icelandic song, this time there are three time signatures.

38 Farmyard Cantata

Icelandic Folk Song

Hen and dog and   pig and goose, horse and mouse and   don - key,

cack- le, bark and squeak and squawk, neigh and bray and   sing   all   day.

38

Folksongs are songs which have been handed down over the centuries. No one knows who composed them, some of them are very old indeed.

Don't forget the slur.

39 Riding High and Low

Icelandic Folk Song

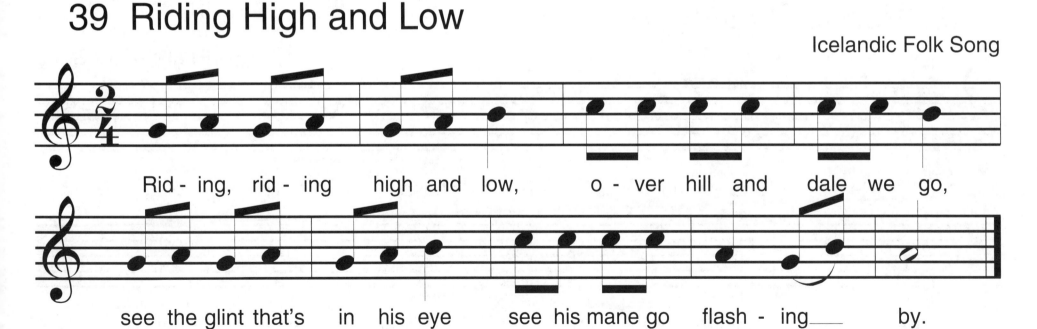

Rid - ing, rid - ing high and low, o - ver hill and dale we go,

see the glint that's in his eye see his mane go flash - ing____ by.

Remember to hold the half notes
for two full counts.

40 Pease Pudding Hot

English Folk Song

Pease pud - ding hot, pease pud - ding cold,

pease pud - ding in the pot four days old!

We can sometimes think of songs being made up of different sections like building bricks. This song is made up of four bricks, three are just the same, one is different.

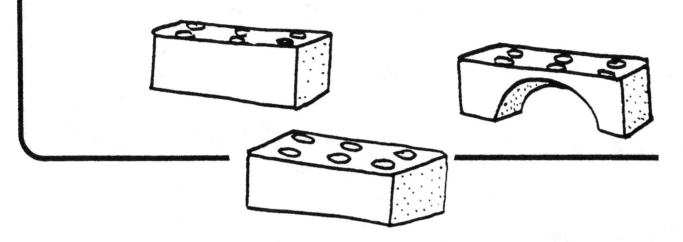
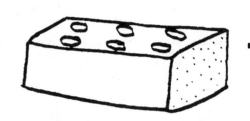

41 Just the Same

Swedish folk song

Just the same play the game, this one is - n't quite the same.

This is a half note rest. You count two just like a half note.

42 Mary Had a Little Lamb

English Song

Ma - ry had a lit - tle lamb, lit - tle lamb, lit - tle lamb,

Ma - ry had a lit - tle lamb its fleece was white as snow.

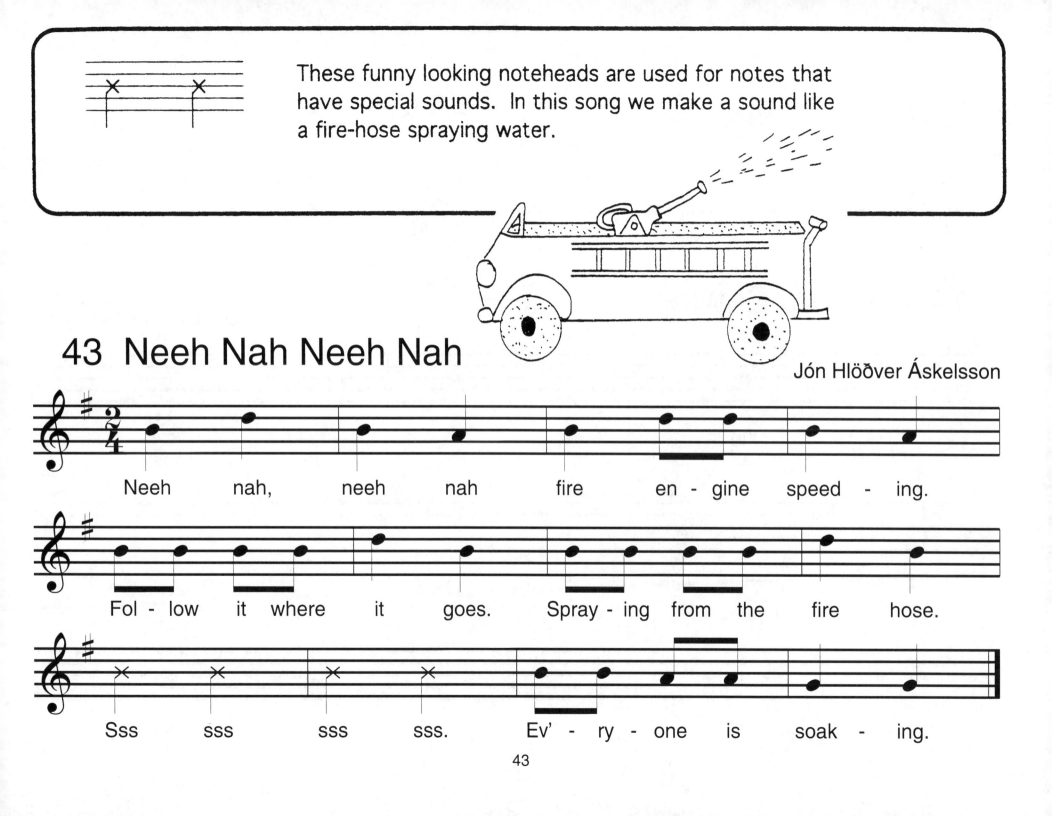

These funny looking noteheads are used for notes that have special sounds. In this song we make a sound like a fire-hose spraying water.

43 Neeh Nah Neeh Nah

Jón Hlöðver Áskelsson

Neeh nah, neeh nah fire en - gine speed - ing.

Fol - low it where it goes. Spray - ing from the fire hose.

Sss sss sss sss. Ev' - ry - one is soak - ing.

43

This is a repeat sign.

44 Sawing, Sawing

Jón Hlöðver Áskelsson

Saw - ing down the big tree.
Come a - long and help me.

Pull and push the saw with me.
'Till we fell the great big tree.

Soon we'll have a bon - fire.

44

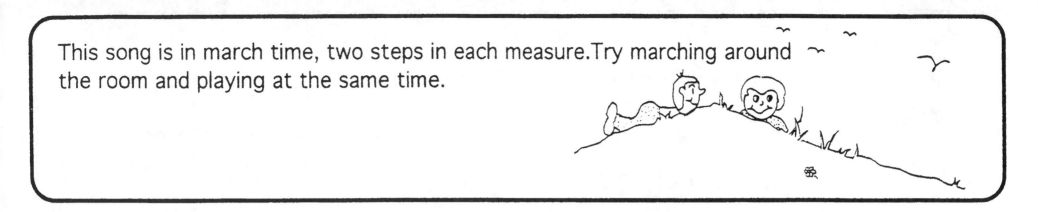

This song is in march time, two steps in each measure. Try marching around the room and playing at the same time.

45 Birds in May

German folk song

Birds in May sing all day, all the chil - dren laugh and play.

Spring is here flowers ap - pear, all is bright and gay.

Birds are sing - ing in the trees, grass - es blow - ing in the breeze.

Birds in May sing all day, all the chil - dren play.

These are sixteenth notes, they are quite fast.

Say "tirrytee"

46 Magnus Sings

Icelandic folk song

Mag- nus sings the church_ bell rings the fox is on the hill.

Birds are sing - ing bells_ are ring - ing lit - tle lambs are still.

A strange old Icelandic rhyme which really doesn't make a lot of sense in either English or Icelandic. Children's rhymes are often like that.

47 Raven Sitting on the Wall

Icelandic folk song

Ra - ven sit-ting up - on the wall, pick-ing his hor - ny toes, but he won't get an-y din-ner to - day, that's the way it goes. 'Cause___ twelve sheep are gone, yes twelve sheep are gone, no, he won't get a-ny din-ner to - day 'cause twelve sheep are gone.

Be careful to stand or sit correctly when you play.
Don't push your shoulders back, that will make you
stiff in the neck.

48 I Shall Sing a Lullaby

Icelandic folk song

Go to sleep my   lit - tle one,   I   will sing a   lul - la - by,

wait   for Dad - dy,   he has gone   out   to catch some   fish to   fry.

The dot behind the note makes it longer.
Half notes become three beats long
instead of two.

49 Winter Goodbye

German folk song

Win - ter good - bye, win - ter good - bye.

Slow - ly the snow melts a - way spring sun is warm - ing the day.

Win - ter good - bye, win - ter good - bye.

If you sit to play your recorder, don't rest your elbows on the table, or you will make yourself stiff and tired in the neck and shoulders.

50 The First Day of Spring

Icelandic folk song

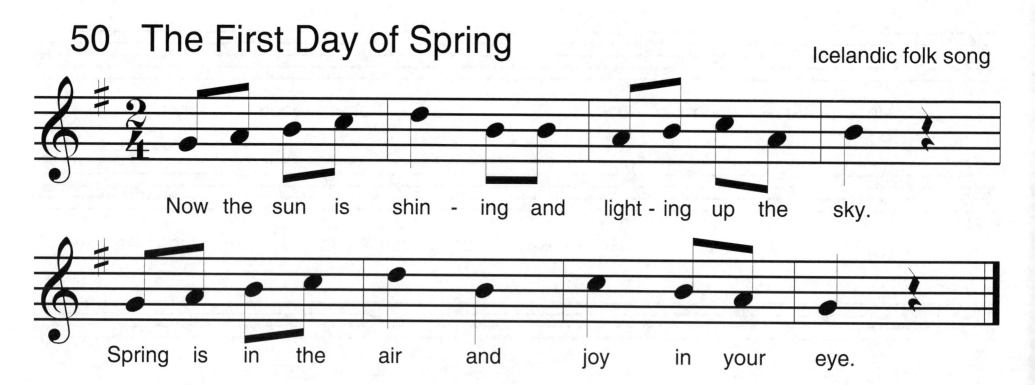

Now the sun is shin - ing and light - ing up the sky.

Spring is in the air and joy in your eye.

This sign means "common time" and is just the same as 4/4.

51 Hot Cross Buns!

English Nursery Rhyme

Hot cross buns! Hot cross buns! One - a - pen - ny two - a - pen - ny

hot cross buns. Give them to you daugh - ters give them to your sons.

One - a - pen - ny two - a - pen - ny hot cross buns.

Don't forget to hold whole notes for a count of four.

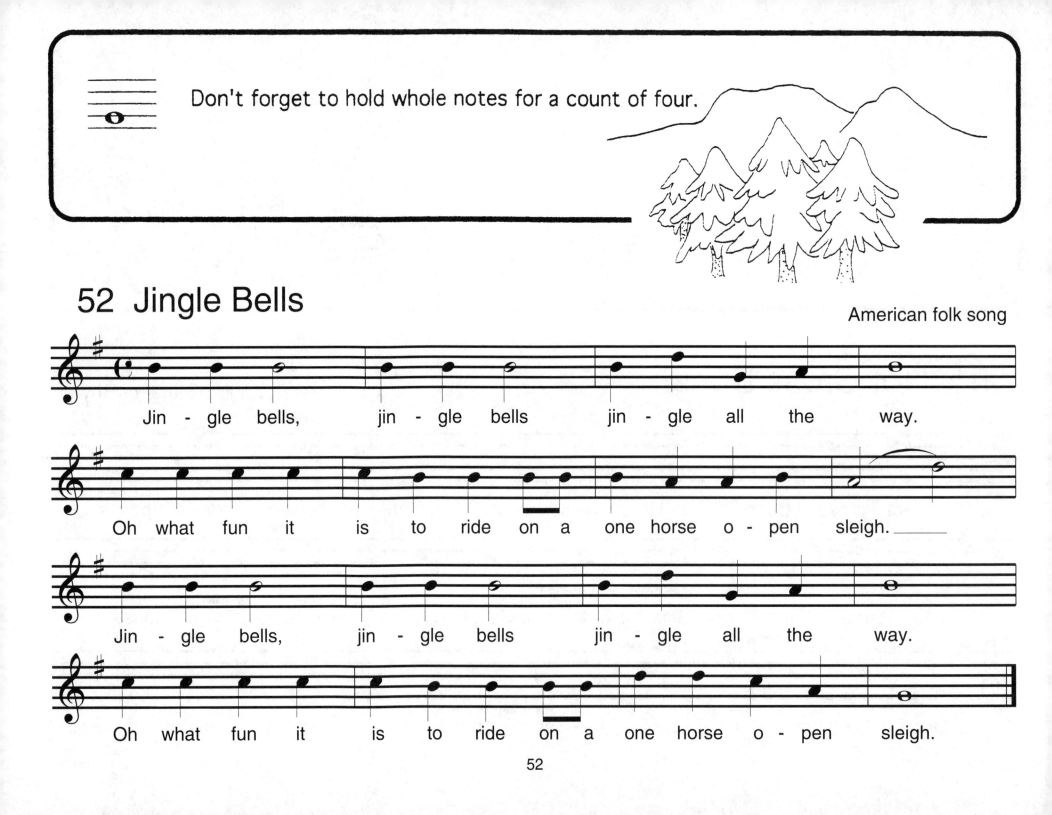

52 Jingle Bells

American folk song

Jin - gle bells, jin - gle bells jin - gle all the way.

Oh what fun it is to ride on a one horse o - pen sleigh. ____

Jin - gle bells, jin - gle bells jin - gle all the way.

Oh what fun it is to ride on a one horse o - pen sleigh.

Now we get to play with both hands. All the songs in the next book use both hands.

E

53 Little Bird

Anonymous

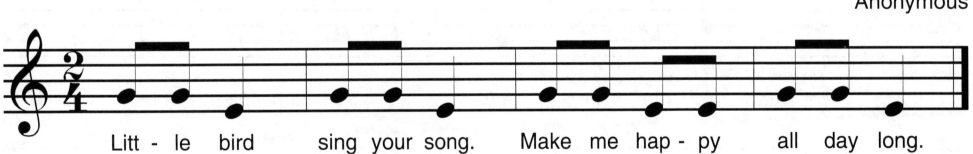

Litt - le bird sing your song. Make me hap - py all day long.

This is a rather sad song. It is played slowly.
The Italian word for that is Largo.

54   Little Dappled Pony

Hungarian Song

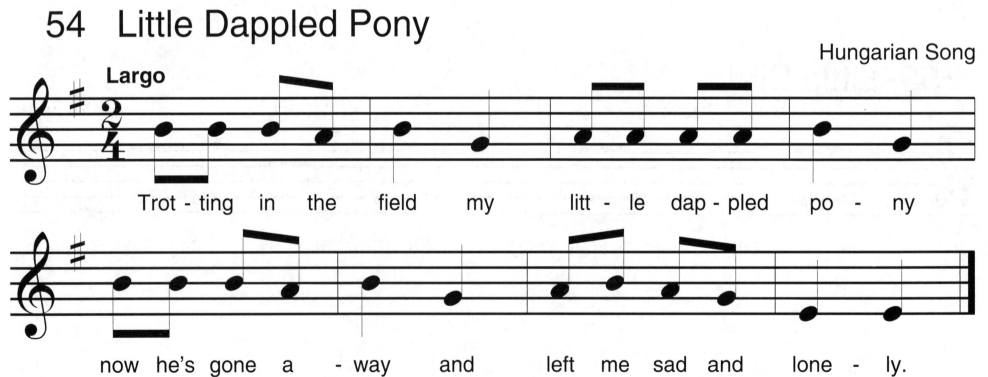

Largo

Trot - ting   in   the   field   my   litt - le   dap - pled   po - ny

now   he's   gone   a   - way   and   left   me   sad   and   lone - ly.

Some songs are quite fast.
The name for that is "allegro."

55 The Little Indian

American Song

Allegro

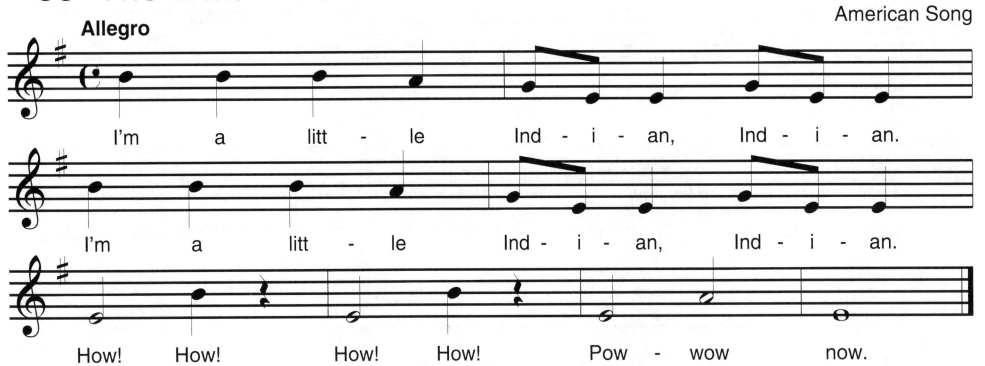

I'm a litt - le Ind - i - an, Ind - i - an.

I'm a litt - le Ind - i - an, Ind - i - an.

How! How! How! How! Pow - wow now.

It's easy to get lost when playing repeats. How many measure are there all together counting repeated ones?

56 My Best Cow

Norwegian folk song

If you have some bells or chime bars you can play the Chinese bells everytime you see these notes. Get a friend or Mom and Dad to play them with you. Can you find two that sound these notes?

57 Chinese Bells

Chinese folk song

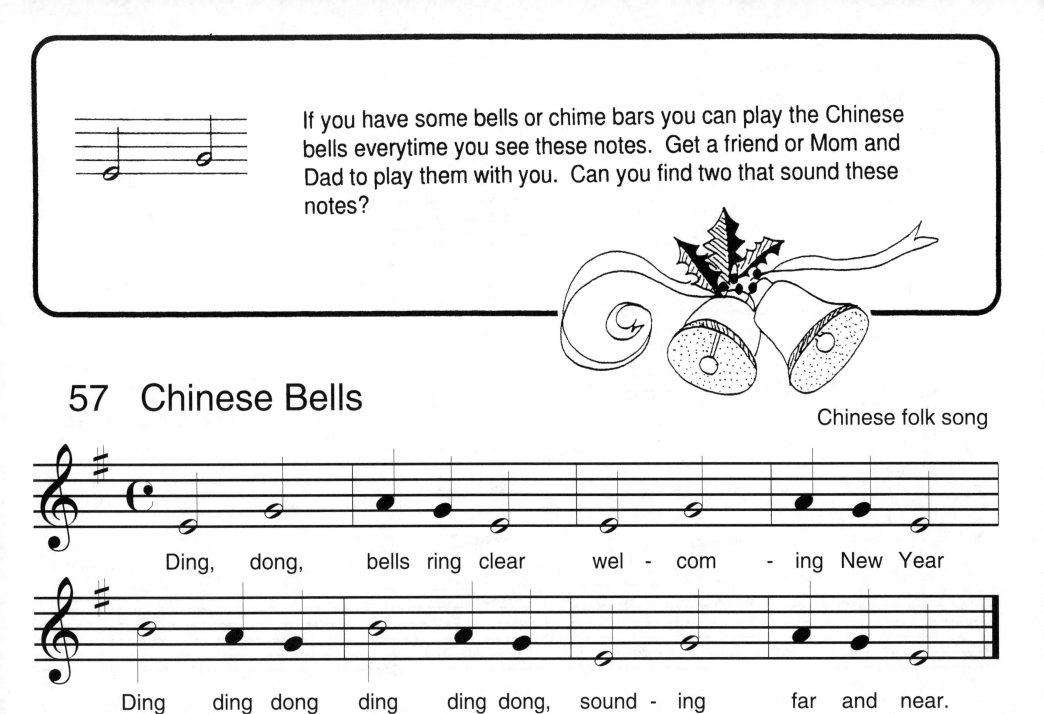

Ding,   dong,   bells ring clear   wel - com   - ing New Year

Ding   ding dong   ding   ding dong,   sound - ing   far and near.

Try playing the songs by ear.
Try playing them with your
eyes closed.

58 Midnight Sunrise

Folk Song from Israel

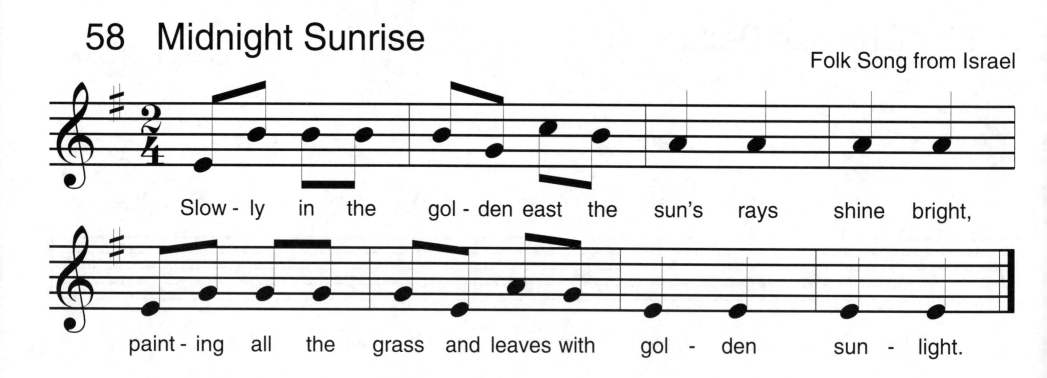

Slow - ly in the gol - den east the sun's rays shine bright,

paint - ing all the grass and leaves with gol - den sun - light.

Dots behind notes make them longer.

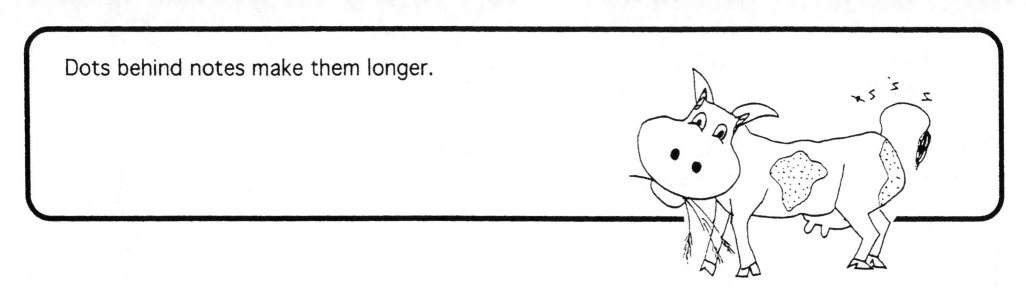

59 Moo Cow

Anonymous

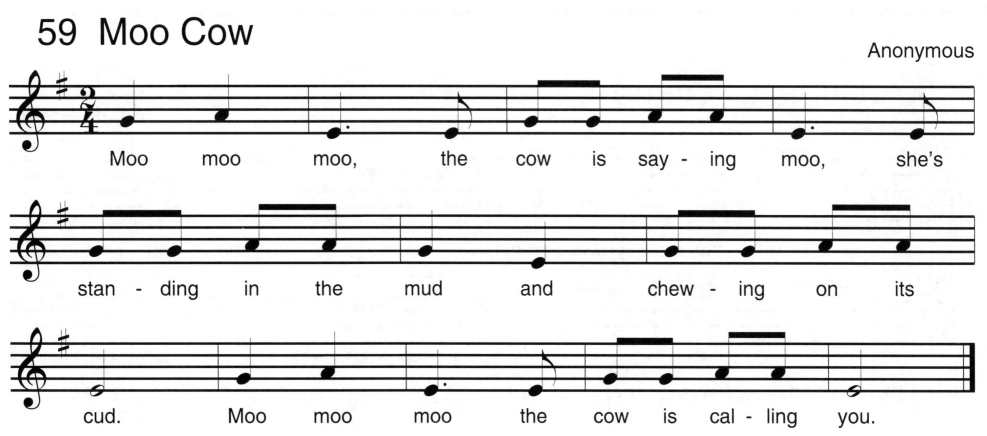

Moo   moo   moo,   the   cow   is   say - ing   moo,   she's

stan - ding   in   the   mud   and   chew - ing   on   its

cud.   Moo   moo   moo   the   cow   is   cal - ling   you.

Try playing together with a friend. Let them play one line, and then you the next. Can you make another part that fits?

When you can play all these songs you are ready for the next book, Mel Bay's Children's Recorder Method Book 2.

60 Come on Home

Jón Ásgeirsson

Come on home and have some tea sit - ting at the ta - ble.

Come and play this song with me, play it if you're a - ble.

About the Authors

Sigurlína Jónsdóttir and Michael Jón Clarke live and work in the beautiful town of Akureyri in north Iceland. Michael is a qualified Suzuki violin teacher, conductor, choir director and opera singer. He has studied in England and the U.S. Sigurlína, a violist, studied in Iceland and the U.S. and has nearly two decades of experience teaching preschool and first grade music. Children's Recorder Method Volume 1 is an English adaptation of their highly successful "Flautað til Leiks" which is taught extensively in Iceland, and loved by teachers and pupils alike.